To,
Dan,
Happy R

The Magic Puzzle

Written & illustrated by Inderjit Puaar

Bradley the Bus lived in London. "I'm so bored," moaned Bradley.

"Would you like to find pieces of my magic puzzle? I have six pieces but three are missing," explained Grandpa.

"**BEEP BEEP!** A magic puzzle! Sure!" said Bradley and off he went.

Grandpa told Bradley that the puzzle was very old. The three missing pieces were in Egypt, India and China, all ancient places.

"Egypt is so far away and I get sea sick. I hope my friends will help me," said Bradley.

"**BEEP BEEP!** First stop, Egypt," hooted Bradley. "Hello Jamilia. Can you please help me find a piece of my magic puzzle?" asked Bradley.

"A magic puzzle! Sure!" said Jamilia the Jeep and off they went.

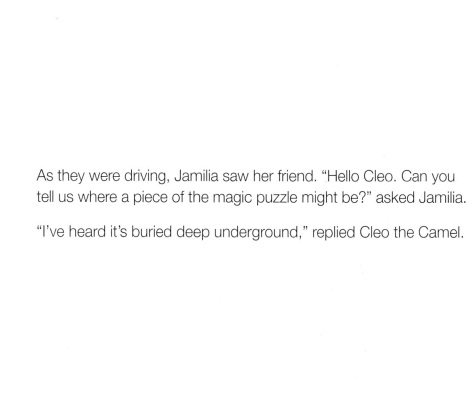

As they were driving, Jamilia saw her friend. "Hello Cleo. Can you tell us where a piece of the magic puzzle might be?" asked Jamilia.

"I've heard it's buried deep underground," replied Cleo the Camel.

"We have been driving for hours," sighed Bradley. "Look! Those tracks lead into that tunnel. I am going inside," said Bradley boldly.

"Bradley, you are so brave! I will wait here," replied Jamilia.

Bradley drove deep underground and saw a glimmer of light.

"**BEEP BEEP!** I found it! I wonder why there's a bird on this piece," said Bradley, who was dazzled by the magic piece of the puzzle.

Bradley thanked Jamilia. "Now to my second stop, India. I wish I could fly there," imagined Bradley, and suddenly he started flying!

"**BEEP BEEP!** The piece of the puzzle has given me magic power to fly like a bird," said Bradley happily as he flew to India.

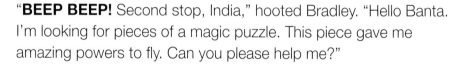

"**BEEP BEEP!** Second stop, India," hooted Bradley. "Hello Banta. I'm looking for pieces of a magic puzzle. This piece gave me amazing powers to fly. Can you please help me?"

"A magic puzzle! Sure!" said Banta the Bus and off they went.

"Grandpa gave me a clue, **T_J MAHA_**," Bradley told Banta.
"Could it be TEJ MAHAK? No. TOJ MAHAI? No, of course!
It's the **TAJ MAHAL!**" exclaimed Bradley.

"All that flying has made me hungry, let's eat before we go," said
Bradley, but as he was eating he accidently bit into a green chilli.

"**BEEEEPPP!**" he hooted. It was so hot, steam burst out of his tyres!

Bradley soon felt better and off they went to the Taj Mahal.

"I think the Taj Mahal is this way," said Banta, but soon they were lost.

"**ROOOAARR!**" a tiger growled and they both jumped with fright. "My name is Taran. Don't worry, I will help you," said Taran the Tiger.

"Phew!" said Bradley with relief, and Taran led them to the Taj Mahal.

"It's so beautiful," gasped Bradley as they arrived at the Taj Mahal. He looked in the water and there was the next piece of the puzzle!

"**BEEP BEEP!** I found it! It has a picture of water on it. Thanks Banta. Now on to my third stop, China," said Bradley, and flew to China.

"**BEEP BEEP!** Third stop, China!" hooted Bradley. "Hello Cheng. I'm looking for pieces of a magic puzzle. Can you help?" asked Bradley.

"A magic puzzle! Sure!" said Cheng the Coach.

It was Chinese New Year and Bradley spotted a dragon mask. "**ROAR!**" joked Bradley.

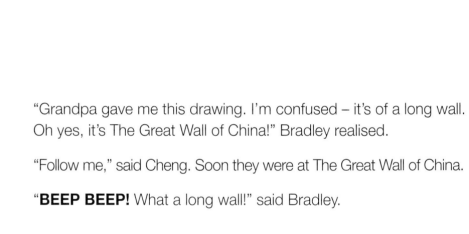

"Grandpa gave me this drawing. I'm confused – it's of a long wall. Oh yes, it's The Great Wall of China!" Bradley realised.

"Follow me," said Cheng. Soon they were at The Great Wall of China.

"**BEEP BEEP!** What a long wall!" said Bradley.

Whilst driving, Bradley saw a loose brick. Behind it was the last piece of the magic puzzle!

"**BEEP BEEP!** I found it! There are oblongs on this piece," said Bradley

Bradley thanked Cheng and flew all the way back to London.

Bradley told his grandpa all about his adventure, and showed him the three pieces of the puzzle. Grandpa joined all the pieces together.

"Well done, Bradley!" said Grandpa proudly. "The puzzle will now give you amazing magic powers when you touch each piece."

"**BEEP BEEP!** I can't wait to be a super bus!" said Bradley happily.

... and now the magic begins.

Stop, Look, Listen, Think

- We need to **HOLD HANDS** when outside
- We must always **STOP** before crossing the road
- We must **LOOK** all around for traffic before crossing the road
- We need to **BE SEEN** when out near traffic
- We must always **LISTEN** carefully before we cross the road
- We must make sure all traffic has stopped before using a **ZEBRA CROSSING**
- We must always cross when and where it is **SAFE**
- We must only cross when the **GREEN MAN** shows
- We must always walk on the **PAVEMENT**

The Magic Puzzle

Written & illustrated by Inderjit Puaar

**Join Bradley the Bus on his adventure
to find three missing pieces of a MAGIC puzzle.**

www.bradleythebus.com

 Published by
iNQ Publications

Printed in England

ISBN 978-0-9570867-0-8

Supported by

 Transport
for London

£4.99

9 780957 086708

Bradley
THE • BUS
Zoom to the Moon

Written & illustrated by Inderjit Puaar

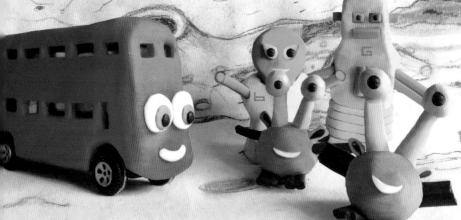

Published by iNQ Publications 2019
27 Old Gloucester Street, London, WC1N 3AX

Text and illustrations copyright © Inderjit Puaar 2019

ISBN 978-0-9570867-1-5

www.bradleythebus.com

Printed in England